Little Women is a gentle story about an ordinary family in the nineteenth century. It was based on the author's own childhood memories, and although it was published as long ago as 1868, it has proved a favourite with generation after generation of girls ever since.

British Library Cataloguing in Publication Data
Collins, Joan, *1917—*
    Little Women by Louisa M. Alcott.—(Children's classics).
    I. Title   II. Gabbey, Terry
    III. Alcott, Louisa M.   IV. Series
    823'.914 J   PZ7
    ISBN 0-7214-0998-9

First edition
Published by Ladybird Books Ltd Loughborough Leicestershire UK
Ladybird Books Inc Lewiston Maine 04240 USA
© LADYBIRD BOOKS LTD MCMLXXXVII
Printed in England

LITTLE WOMEN

by Louisa M Alcott

retold by Joan Collins
illustrated by Terry Gabbey

Ladybird Books

Meg, Jo, Beth, and Amy

'Christmas won't be Christmas without any presents,' grumbled Jo, stretching out her long legs on the hearth rug.

'It's dreadful to be poor!' sighed Meg, looking down at her shabby dress.

'I don't think it's fair for some girls to have everything and other girls nothing at all,' added little Amy with a sniff.

'We've got Father and Mother and each other,' said Beth contentedly, from her corner.

The firelight flickered over the faces of the four sisters as they sat knitting in the cosy room. The December snow was falling gently outside the window, and inside there was an atmosphere of home and peace.

But Jo said sadly, 'We haven't got Father, and shan't have him for a very long time.' The girls' father, Mr March, was too old to fight in

4

the American Civil War, so he had volunteered to be an army chaplain. The girls were very proud of him.

It was going to be a hard winter for everyone, especially for the men in the army. The girls' mother, whom they called Marmee, thought they ought not to spend any money on presents for themselves that Christmas. '*We* should give up something, too,' she had said.

The girls were disappointed. They had looked forward to spending their hard-earned pocket money. Jo had planned to buy a favourite book, Beth some piano music, and Amy, the artistic one, drawing pencils.

'We do deserve *some* fun,' said Jo. 'After all, we work hard enough.'

'I know I do,' said Meg, the pretty one, who was sixteen. She was nursery governess to a family of naughty children. Jo, the fifteen-year-old tomboy, went every day to look after her cross, elderly aunt. Shy Beth, thirteen, stayed at home. Amy, eleven and the youngest, was still at school.

Jo sat up and shook her thick chestnut hair out of its net. 'If only I'd been born a boy!' she cried. 'Then I could go and fight in the army with Father, instead of staying at home and knitting soldiers' socks!'

'Never mind, Jo,' said Beth. 'You must be content with being the man of the family while Father is away.'

The clock struck six, and Beth put her mother's slippers by the fire to warm.

'They're nearly worn out. Marmee needs a new pair,' said Jo.

The girls' faces lit up. Suddenly they knew what to buy with their Christmas money!

'Glad to find you so merry, girls!' said a voice from the doorway. It was Marmee, in her old cloak and plain bonnet, the dearest mother in the world.

Mrs March took off her wet things, put on her warm slippers, and prepared for the happiest hour of the day. 'Sit down,' she said. 'I've a treat for you!' And she patted her pocket.

'A letter from Father!' they all cried.

The letter was cheerful, with no mention of hardships or dangers. Only at the end did their father show how much he missed his daughters. 'When I come back,' he wrote, 'I shall be fonder and prouder than ever of my little women.'

The letter brought tears to the girls' eyes, and they made some resolutions. Jo promised not to be so wild, Amy not to be so selfish, and Meg not to be so vain. Quiet Beth said nothing, but began to knit with all her might!

Mrs March smiled at her daughters. 'Do you remember the game of *Pilgrim's Progress* you played when you were little?' she asked. 'You climbed from the basement, which was the City of Destruction, all the way up to the Celestial City, which was the attic, carrying your burdens.'

'I liked the place where the burdens fell off!' said Meg.

'I liked the cake and milk at the top!' said Amy. 'I wish we weren't too old to play it now.'

'That is a game you play all your lives,' said Marmee wisely. 'See how far you can get on the journey before Father comes home!'

'But what are our burdens?' asked the girls.

'I think you've just told me about them,' said Marmee. 'Jo's wildness, Amy's selfishness, Meg's vanity. Only Beth hasn't told me about hers. I think perhaps she hasn't got any.'

'Mine are dishes and dusters and envying girls with nice pianos, and being afraid of people!' confessed Beth.

Before they went to bed, the girls sang carols together. The quiet, happy music was their Christmas lullaby.

A merry Christmas

When the girls ran down to breakfast on Christmas morning, Marmee wasn't there to greet them.

'There was a poor creetur come a-begging, and your ma went straight off to see what was needed,' said Hannah. Hannah had been with them since they were babies, and was part of the family by now.

The girls put their mother's presents on the table and waited eagerly for her return. At last the door banged, and in she came.

'There is a woman nearby with a little newborn baby,' she said. 'She has six children huddled in one bed to keep warm. They have no food or fire. Will you give them your breakfast as a Christmas present?'

The girls did not hesitate. They piled up buckwheat cakes and muffins on plates. Hannah took an armful of wood, and some blankets, and they set off.

Marmee took them to a bare, miserable room, where there was a sick mother, and hungry children crowded together under an old quilt.

'It's good angels come to help us!' cried the poor woman, hugging her baby.

'Funny angels, in hoods and mittens!' laughed Jo, as they fed the children and Hannah built a fire.

Back at home, they gave Marmee her new slippers and had bread and milk for breakfast.

*   *   *

Jo had written a play for the girls to put on for their friends at Christmas. It was an 'operatic tragedy' about a witch, a villain, and a pair of lovers. The props and costumes were all homemade, and the performance was held in the old barn next to the house.

Jo played all the male roles, in a treasured pair of thigh boots, an old tunic, and a slouch hat. Meg, in a grey wig, was the witch, and Amy was the golden-haired heroine. Beth played all the minor parts, and kept forgetting her lines.

All went well until the train of the heroine's dress got caught, just as she was eloping from a 'tower' of piled-up chairs. Both she and the tower came crashing to the floor. A pair of leather boots waved wildly in the ruins, and a golden head appeared, shrieking, 'I told you so!'

At the end of the play, there was loud applause from the 'dress circle'. This was a cot-bed, which folded up unexpectedly and shut the audience up inside it! Luckily, Hannah came in at that moment to call everyone in to supper.

The girls' eyes opened wide when they saw the magnificent spread. There were two kinds of ice cream, cake, fruit, and sweets, all decorated with hothouse flowers. Their next-door neighbour, rich old Mr Laurence, had been *their* 'good angel'. He had heard of the morning's doings, and sent 'a few trifles for the girls in honour of the day.' It certainly made up for the bread-and-milk breakfast!

'That boy put it into his head!' cried Jo, who had met the old man's grandson,

Laurie, when he had returned their runaway cat.

Old Mr Laurence did not mix much with his neighbours, and kept his young grandson inside, hard at work at lessons with his tutor.

'I mean to make friends with that boy one day,' Jo decided. 'I know he needs some fun!'

'I wish we could send some of these flowers to Father,' said Beth wistfully. 'I'm afraid he isn't having as merry a Christmas as we are!'

Burdens

'I wish it were Christmas all the time!' said Jo, when the holidays were over.

Everyone seemed out of sorts at breakfast that morning. Beth had a headache, Jo had broken her shoelace, Amy had not done her homework. Poor Mrs March was trying to write a letter amidst all the confusion.

At last the girls set off to begin their day's work – to take up their 'burdens'.

* * *

Jo's burden was fetching and carrying for crotchety old Aunt March, who was lame and needed help at home. Jo disliked the work, but she loved the large library, left to dust and spiders since Uncle March died. The moment Aunt March took a nap, Jo hurried off to the dim room and curled up in an armchair to read.

But always, when she got to the most interesting part, a shrill voice would call, 'Josy-phine!' and she would have to go and wash the poodle, feed the parrot, wind wool, or read something dull and tedious to her aunt.

*   *   *

Meg was old enough to remember the pleasant life at home before their father had lost all his money trying to help a friend. It was hard for her to have to work now, and especially hard to work for the rich King family. She envied the King girls their parties and new dresses, while she had to look after the spoiled younger children.

But that day there was trouble in the King family. Mrs King was crying, Mr King was shouting, and the girls were silent. The eldest son had done something to disgrace the family. Perhaps dresses and parties weren't everything, Meg thought.

* * *

Beth had her lessons at home and helped Hannah. She spent quiet days alone, busy with chores, or caring tenderly for her three kittens. She also had six battered old dolls that she loved, and nursed as if they were invalids.

Beth's secret sorrow was that she could not have music lessons. She practised patiently on the jingly old piano, with its yellow keys that would never keep in tune, hoping that 'one day I'll get my music, if I'm good!'

*   *   *

Amy's burden was her rather flat nose. She wished it were 'aristocratic', and she drew page after page of handsome noses to comfort herself.

Amy was popular with her school friends. They admired her little airs and graces and the long words she used (not always the right ones!) She could have been spoiled, but her vanity was kept in check because she had to wear her cousin's cast-off dresses. That winter, her school dress was a dull purple with yellow dots. It offended Amy's artistic taste!

*   *   *

That evening, the girls brought back tales of their day's activities. Marmee listened, gently guiding them to see how lucky they were in their happy family life, even though they could not have everything they wanted.

The Laurence boy

The March family's house was separated by a hedge from the Laurences' stately stone mansion. The Laurence house was a lonely place, where no children played and almost no one but the old gentleman and his grandson went in and out.

Jo imagined the house to be a palace of delights with nobody to enjoy them. And she had long wanted to make friends with 'the Laurence boy'.

One snowy afternoon, as she was clearing a path round the garden, she saw old Mr Laurence drive off. She quickly dug her way down to the hedge. All was quiet. But, at an upstairs window, she saw a dark curly head leaning on a thin hand.

Jo tossed a snowball up.

Laurie's face brightened at once, and he opened the window.

'I've got a bad cold. I've been in bed for a week,' he croaked.

'You need some company!' said Jo cheerfully.

'So I do! Would you come up?'

'I must ask Marmee first,' said Jo, and ran off into her house.

When she returned, she was carrying Beth's kittens and a dish of Meg's blancmange, decorated with flowers from Amy's pet geranium. 'Everyone wanted to do something!' she said. She swept the hearth and plumped up the cushions to make the room cosy.

Then they began to talk. Jo made Laurie laugh with tales of Aunt March and her parrot that spoke Spanish. Laurie wanted to know all about Jo's family. He often watched them at night, gathered round their mother in the lamplight. Laurie had no mother. Jo could tell he was lonely.

'I wish you'd come over, instead of peeping,' she said. 'We'd have such a jolly time!'

When old Mr Laurence came back, Jo found that he was not nearly as frightening as she had imagined. He told her he had been a friend of her grandfather, and showed her his splendid library.

'What have you been doing to this boy of mine?' he asked her over tea.

'Trying to cheer him up!' Jo said. 'I think he could do with some young company.'

Mr Laurence watched the two laughing and talking together. 'She's right,' he thought. 'The lad is lonely. I'll see what these girls can do for him.' He liked Jo's blunt ways, and she seemed to understand the boy.

A little later, Laurie played on the grand piano. Jo wished Beth could hear him.

When she went home, with an armful of hothouse flowers, she told her family all about her afternoon. They all longed to go to the great house and see its treasures for themselves.

'I was thinking about *Pilgrim's Progress*,' said Beth dreamily. 'When Christian got up the steep hill, he came to the Palace Beautiful. Maybe the house over there is going to be *our* Palace Beautiful.'

'We've got to get past the lions first!' said Jo.

Beth finds the Palace Beautiful

The big house did prove a Palace Beautiful, though Beth found it very hard to pass the lions. For her, the biggest lion was old Mr Laurence. After he had called and had a kind word with the girls, and talked over old times with their mother, Beth was the only one who was still afraid of him.

Everyone liked Laurie, and even Beth was not shy with him. His tutor, Mr Brooke, complained that he was always playing truant now and running over to the Marches. 'Never mind!' said his grandfather. 'He deserves a holiday, and he won't come to any harm over there.'

So there was skating, and there were sleigh rides and plays and fun.

At the Laurence house, Jo had the freedom of the library, Meg loved the hothouse, and Amy copied the pictures. But Beth was too shy to touch the grand piano. Mr Laurence noticed this. One day he asked Mrs March if any of her girls would like to come over and practise – 'to keep the piano in tune.'

'They needn't *see* anybody,' he said slyly. 'I'm always shut up in my study in the evenings, and there are no servants about. But if the girls don't care to, never mind.'

A little hand slipped timidly into his. 'Oh, sir, they *do* care, very much!' said Beth.

Mr Laurence looked down. Beth's blue eyes reminded him of his little granddaughter who had died, and his heart softened even more.

After that, Beth came to play the piano nearly every day. Mr Laurence made sure no one disturbed her. And he often left his study door open, to hear the sweet music she made.

Beth decided to embroider a pair of slippers with pansies for Mr Laurence, as a thank-you present. Imagine her joy and surprise when, the next day, a beautiful little cabinet piano was delivered 'for Miss Elizabeth March'. It had belonged to Mr Laurence's granddaughter. With it was a note. 'Heart's-ease is my favourite flower,' it said, and it was signed, 'Your grateful friend and humble servant, James Laurence.'

'You'll have to go over and thank him,' teased Jo, never dreaming Beth would have the courage to do it.

But she surprised them all. She marched straight over to the house next door, climbed up on Mr Laurence's knee, and kissed him.

'I do believe the world is coming to an end!' Meg gasped.

Beth was never afraid of Mr Laurence again.

Jo meets her dark angel

'Girls, where are you going?' asked Amy, coming into their room one Saturday afternoon and finding Meg and Jo ready to go out.

'Never mind! Little girls shouldn't ask questions,' answered Jo sharply.

Amy's feelings were hurt. She had been feeling very left out of things lately. Jo was always with Laurie, Beth had her piano, and Meg was growing up into a 'young lady'.

It turned out that Laurie was taking Meg and Jo to see a play called 'The Seven Castles of the Diamond Lake'. Amy wanted to go, too. She began to cry, but Jo refused to take her. 'It would spoil everything!' she said.

'You'll be sorry for this, Jo March!' called Amy over the banisters, as the girls went out.

'Fiddlesticks!' said Jo, slamming the door.

When they got home, Amy was sitting in the parlour, reading. She did not ask a single question about the play. Jo was suspicious.

She went upstairs and looked round her room to see what mischief Amy had done, but everything was in order.

Next day, however, Jo discovered that a little book of fairy stories she had written was missing. She had worked on the book lovingly for a year, and it was her only copy.

Jo pounced on Amy. 'You've got it!' she said.

'Scold as much as you like, you'll never see it again! I burned it up!' cried Amy triumphantly. 'I said I'd pay you back!'

'What? My little book I was so fond of and meant to finish before Father came home?' Jo turned pale and shook Amy till her teeth chattered. 'I'll never forgive you, *never*!'

Even when Amy said she was sorry, Jo would not make friends.

As she kissed Jo good night, Marmee whispered, 'Don't let the sun go down on your anger, dear. Forgive each other and begin again tomorrow.'

'She doesn't *deserve* to be forgiven!' said Jo gruffly.

*   *   *

Next day was the last day of winter skating. To cheer herself up, Jo went down to the river with Laurie. They had promised to take Amy skating before the ice broke up, but Jo was still cross and went without her.

Amy ran after them, meaning to tell Jo how truly sorry she was. Jo saw her on the bank, struggling with her skates, but took no notice.

Laurie had skated ahead to see if the ice was safe. 'Keep near the bank!' he called. 'It's dangerous in the middle!'

But Amy did not hear him. Jo could see that Amy hadn't heard, but her little demon of temper whispered, 'Let her take care of herself!'

So Amy skated out onto the smoother ice.

Suddenly the ice broke. Amy disappeared.

The next few moments were a nightmare for Jo. At last she and Laurie managed to pull Amy out of the icy water, but she knew that the accident was her fault.

When Amy was safely home, Jo confessed to Marmee. 'It's my dreadful temper!' she cried. 'I try to cure it, but then it breaks out again. What can I do? You don't know how hard it is!'

Marmee put her arms round the sobbing Jo and told her a secret. 'You think your temper is the worst in the world, but mine used to be just like it. I've been trying to control it for forty years!' And she explained how their father had taught her to be patient. She talked lovingly to Jo about forgiveness.

Jo went up to look at Amy in bed, and thought how dreadful it would have been if that golden head had been swept away for ever under the ice. Amy opened her eyes. Her arms went round Jo, and everything was forgotten in one sisterly kiss.

Meg goes to Vanity Fair

One April afternoon, Meg was excitedly packing her best things to go on a visit to her friend Sallie Moffat. The sisters all gathered round her, offering to lend her their treasures.

Meg's simple outfit looked nearly perfect to their eyes, but Meg was doubtful about her old party dress of white muslin. 'It isn't low-necked, and it doesn't sweep enough,' she sighed, 'but it will have to do.'

'Never mind! You always look like an angel in white,' said Amy, looking enviously at Meg's silk stockings, pretty fan and *two* pairs of gloves.

The Moffats were fashionable folk, and Meg was dazzled by the splendour of their house. They were kind, and gave her what they called 'a good time' – shopping, entertaining, and paying calls.

On the evening of the party, Meg realised how limp and shabby her white dress looked alongside the other girls' crisp new silks. She felt miserable, until a box of beautiful flowers arrived from Laurie. Meg generously divided them up into posies for all her friends. Then she happily fastened roses to the neck of her white dress, which did not seem half so shabby now.

Meg enjoyed herself that evening. She heard one of the guests, Major Lincoln, ask who 'the fresh little girl with the beautiful eyes' was, and she was asked to sing.

Then everything was spoiled.

Meg overheard Mrs Moffat and some of her friends gossiping in the conservatory about the flowers Laurie had sent.

'It would be a grand thing for one of those girls! Sallie says the old man quite dotes on them.'

'Mrs M has made her plans, I dare say!'

'Would she mind if we lent her a dress for Thursday? That dowdy muslin is all she has got.'

'We'll ask young Laurence, as a favour to her,' said Mrs Moffat.

Meg was horrified to hear them speak so of her mother, and of the March family's innocent friendship with Laurie.

Next day, she was told of the invitation to 'Mr Laurence'.

'It's very kind of you,' she said mischievously, 'but I'm afraid he won't come.'

'Why not?'

'He's too old — nearly seventy!'

'We meant the *young* Mr Laurence, of course!'

'Oh, he's only a *boy*!' laughed Meg.

*   *   *

Laurie did come, encouraged by the March family, who wanted to know how Meg looked. But he was disappointed when he saw her. She had allowed the Moffat girls to dress her up like a doll. She wore a low-cut blue silk dress of Sallie's, silver bracelets and earrings, and a pair of high-heeled blue silk boots. They had frizzled her hair and given her cheeks a dusting of powder and rouge.

'Don't you like it?' said Meg, waving her plumy fan.

'I don't like fuss and feathers,' said Laurie honestly.

Meg stalked away to the window to cool her flushed cheeks. Major Lincoln came by with his mother. 'They are making a fool of that girl,' he said. 'I wanted you to see her, but they have spoiled her entirely.'

'Oh, dear,' sighed Meg. 'I'm so ashamed of myself!' She begged Laurie not to tell Marmee how she had behaved and looked. 'I want to tell her myself,' she said.

And she did confess to Marmee, and told her about the gossip she had overheard. '*Do* you have "plans" for us, Marmee?' asked Meg.

'Yes, my dear. All mothers do. But mine are different from Mrs Moffat's. I *am* ambitious for my girls, but not for them to marry rich men just because they are rich. Better to be happy old maids than unhappy wives! Your father and I hope that our daughters, married or single, will be the pride and comfort of our lives.'

33

Summer doings

When the summer holidays came, the girls begged Marmee to be allowed to do exactly as they liked for a week, and be free of chores. As Marmee foresaw, this was a disaster.

Meg chose to alter (and spoil) her dresses by trimming them up like Sallie Moffat's. Amy sat in the garden in her best dress, drawing, and soon became bored with her own company. Jo read all day and got a headache. Beth forgot to feed her canary, Pip, and it died.

On the last day, both Marmee and Hannah went out, to see how the girls would manage without them.

Jo decided to give a lunch party, and invited Laurie. Unfortunately, a nosy old lady called Miss Crocker invited herself, too. Jo's choice of lobster, asparagus, and salad, with homemade bread, sounded wonderful. But the asparagus boiled away to nothing, the bread burned, and Jo could not get the meat out of the lobster. At last she served the dessert, which looked very pretty – rosy islands of strawberries, floating in cream and dusted with sugar. Laurie took a mouthful, gulped, and chewed manfully on.

'What's wrong?' cried Jo.

'Salt instead of sugar, and the cream's sour!' gasped Meg. They all burst out laughing, and the meal ended with bread and butter, cold meat, and fun.

When Marmee returned, she told them that she and Hannah had gone out on purpose. 'Now you see what happens when everyone thinks only of herself. Don't you think it's better when each of us takes her share of daily duties?'

'We do, Mother, we do,' chorused the girls.

'From now on we'll work like bees,' said Jo. 'I'm going to learn plain cooking for my holiday task!'

*   *   *

Laurie had guests visiting from England during the summer, and the high spot of the season was a whole day's boating picnic to entertain them. The visitors were amazed at the energy of the American girls!

A quiet observer at the picnic might have noticed that Laurie's tutor, Mr Brooke, paid special attention to Meg. Laurie noticed this himself, and mentioned it to Jo. She, as protector of the family, was furious at the idea!

A telegram

Autumn came, and the days began to grow chilly.

'November is the most disagreeable month of the year,' said Meg one afternoon, as she and her sisters looked out at the frostbitten garden.

'Two nice things are going to happen right away!' exclaimed Beth. 'Marmee is coming down the street, and Laurie is tramping through the garden. He promised to take us for a drive.'

The two came in, Marmee with her usual question: 'Is there a letter from Father?'

'Is there anything I can do for you, Madam Mother?' Laurie asked.

'Call at the post office and ask if there's a letter, dear,' Marmee said anxiously. 'It's not like Father to be so late.'

A sharp ring of the doorbell interrupted her, and Hannah came in with a letter. 'It's one of them horrible telegraph things,' she said.

At the word 'telegraph' Mrs March snatched it, read the two lines it contained, and dropped back into her chair with a white face. Laurie dashed out for some water. Meg and Hannah supported Marmee, while Jo read aloud, in a frightened voice:

Blank Hospital, Washington

Mrs March:

Your husband is very ill. Come at once.

S Hale

The room was still. The day darkened outside, and the whole world seemed to change. 'It may be too late – oh, children, help me to bear it!' said Mrs March, in a voice they never forgot.

Hannah was the first to recover. 'The Lord keep the dear man! I won't waste time cryin', but git your things ready right away, ma'am!'

Marmee sat up, looking pale but steady. 'She's right!' she said.

The girls hurried to help Marmee to pack. Laurie was sent out to send a telegram saying Marmee would come at once. He was also to leave a note at Aunt March's. Jo knew the money for the journey would have to be borrowed from Aunt March, and she wished she could do something to help.

Then old Mr Laurence came. There was nothing he did not offer, from his own dressing-gown for Mr March to himself as escort for Mrs March. But Mrs March would not hear of it – she knew he was too old and frail to travel – so he left.

A few minutes later, as Meg was carrying a pair of overshoes in one hand and a cup of tea in the other, Mr Brooke came in the door. He offered *his* services to escort Mrs March to Washington. Mr Laurence had some business for him to attend there, he said.

Meg dropped the overshoes, and nearly spilt the cup of tea, putting out her hands to him in gratitude, and John Brooke felt amply repaid.

*   *   *

Everything was arranged. The money came from Aunt March, with a note saying she'd always said their father was a fool to go. Jo saw her mother bite her lips, and knew how she felt. Suddenly, Jo rushed out.

When she came back, looking very strange, she laid a roll of bills on her mother's lap. Twenty-five dollars!

'It's my contribution to helping Father and seeing him home safely,' she said.

'Where did you get it?' everyone asked.

'I earned it. I only sold what was my own.'

Jo took off her bonnet. Her long, thick hair had all been cut short.

'This crop is so comfortable I know I'll never miss it!' she said. 'The barber's wife gave me a lock to keep, but I'll give it to you, Marmee, in memory of past glories!'

Marmee took it and put it away carefully. She only said, 'Thank you, dear,' but something in her face made the girls change the subject.

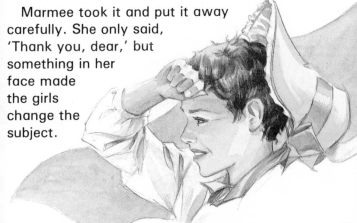

That night, a quiet figure glided from bed to bed, looking at her sleeping daughters. As she lifted the curtain and looked into the dreary night, the moon broke through, as if to whisper, 'Be comforted! There is always light behind the clouds.'

Letters

'I feel as if there had been an earthquake,' said Jo.

'It seems as if half the house has gone,' Meg added forlornly.

Hannah cheered them up briskly and made coffee as a breakfast treat. As they set off for work, there was no Marmee waving goodbye. But Beth had not forgotten them. Her rosy face smiled as she waved to them from the window.

'That's my Beth!' said Jo.

Good news of their father comforted the sisters. Mr Brooke sent regular despatches.

The girls wrote letters of their own to their mother. Jo's were comic:

> *Everyone is so desperately good, it's like living in a nest of turtledoves! You'd laugh to see Meg head the table and try to be motherish!*

Amy complained:

> *Laurie is not as respeckful as he ought to be now I am almost in my teens, he calls me Chick.*

Hannah was blunt:

> *The old gentleman sends heaps of things and means wal, and it aint my place to say nothin. My bread is riz, so no more at this time. I send my duty to Mr March and hope he's seen the last of his Pewmonia.*

Mr Laurence's letter was brief and to the point:

> *Dear Madam,*
> *The little girls are all well. Hannah guards pretty Meg like a dragon. Pray make Brooke useful, and draw on me for funds. Don't let your husband want for anything. Thank God he is mending.*
>
> > *Your sincere friend and servant,*
> > *James Laurence.*

Dark days

'Meg, I wish you or Jo would go to see the poor family we visited at Christmas,' said Beth one day. 'We promised Mother not to forget them, and now their baby is sick.'

But the older girls were tired and put things off, so Beth went. She came back sadly. The baby had died of scarlet fever in Beth's lap. Now Beth had a headache and a sore throat and felt ill.

'If only Mother were at home!' cried Jo.

Jo and Meg had both had scarlet fever, but Amy had not, so she was packed off to Aunt March's.

Beth did have the fever, and was very sick. She talked in a broken voice and played on the quilt as if it were her piano. She did not know anybody, and cried for Marmee. But Mr March was still very ill, and Marmee could not come home.

One day the doctor looked at Beth for a long time. 'If Mrs March can leave her husband, she should be sent for,' he said gravely.

Jo rushed out of the house to send a telegram, and ran full tilt into Laurie.

'Beth mustn't die! I can't give her up, she's my conscience!' Jo sobbed wildly.

'I don't think she will die,' said Laurie, soothing her. 'She's so good, and we all love her so much.' Then he told Jo that he had already telegraphed, and that Marmee was on her way.

'Bless you, Laurie!' Jo cried.

The joyous whisper 'Mother's coming!' ran through the house. The hours dragged by, and night came. At two o'clock Jo bent over Beth's bed. Beth's face was still and pale. Jo thought she was dying.

'Goodbye, Beth, goodbye!' she whispered.

Then Hannah came. 'The fever's turned!' she cried. 'She's sleeping natural!'

When the doctor came that morning, he confirmed the good news. Beth was over the worst. The girls hugged each other and went to sit on the stairs and wait.

'If only Marmee would come,' said Jo.

Suddenly there was a sound of bells at the door, a cry from Hannah, and Laurie's voice: 'Girls! She's come! She's come!'

Problems

There are no words to describe the reunion of the mother and daughters. When Beth woke from that long healing sleep, the first thing she saw was her mother's face.

Laurie went off to give the good news to Amy, who had learned much at Aunt March's. When her mother came to see her, Amy was wearing a pretty ring that Aunt March had given her, but not just as an ornament. 'It's to remind me not to be selfish,' Amy said.

Jo had her problems, too. She resented the place John Brooke had taken in her family's affections, especially in relation to Meg. John had fallen in love with Meg and wanted to marry her.

But Meg was still very young, and not sure of her own feelings. She was confused and upset when John proposed.

Then Aunt March took a hand. She came to the house and told Meg she would be a fool to marry a poor man — and she would leave her nothing in her will if she did!

Meg defended Mr Brooke bravely. 'I shall marry whom I please, Aunt March. And you can leave your money to anyone you like!'

'I couldn't help overhearing, Meg,' said John, who had come by to get an umbrella he had left. 'So you *do* care for me a bit!'

'Yes, John,' said Meg meekly, hiding her face in his waistcoat. 'I didn't realise how much, before!'

Christmas once more

Before the Christmas dinner came the presents. Meg got a silk dress at last, and Jo the book she had always wanted. But the best gift of all was announced by Laurie at the door: 'Here's another Christmas present for the March family!'

A tall man, muffled up to his ears, came in, leaning on the arm of another tall man. Everyone rushed to hug him. 'Hush! Remember Beth!' Marmee cried – but it was too late. The door flew open, and little Beth, in her red wrapper, flew straight into her father's arms.

There never was
such a Christmas dinner.
After it, Mr March looked round at his 'little women'. He saw how each had grown up. Meg was more womanly, Jo less boyish, Amy more thoughtful of others, and Beth not so shy.

'What are you thinking, Beth?' asked Jo.

'I read in *Pilgrim's Progress* how, after many troubles, Christian and Hopeful came into pleasant meadows,' Beth said, 'and they sang this song. It's Father's favourite.'

Beth went to her piano and sang in her sweet voice:

> 'He that is down need fear no fall,
>   He that is low, no pride,
> He that is humble ever shall
>   Have God to be his guide.'

Father and Mother sat together, while Amy sketched the lovers, Meg and John. Beth talked to her old friend, Mr Laurence, while Jo lounged on her favourite seat. Laurie, smiling, leaned on the back of Jo's chair.

So grouped, the curtain falls on Meg, Jo, Beth, and Amy. Whether it ever rises again depends on the reception given to the first act of the domestic drama called *Little Women*.

Louisa M Alcott did continue the story of the March family, which you can read in the books called *Good Wives*, *Jo's Boys*, and *Little Men*.

Stories . . .
that have stood the test of time

SERIES 740
LADYBIRD CHILDREN'S CLASSICS

Treasure Island

Swiss Family Robinson

Secret Garden

A Journey to the
Centre of the Earth

The Three Musketeers

Gulliver's Travels

The Lost World

King Solomon's Mines

Around the World
in Eighty Days

A Christmas Carol

The Wind in the Willows

The Last of the Mohicans

The Happy Prince
and other stories

Peter Pan

Oliver Twist

The Railway Children

Kidnapped

A Little Princess

Black Beauty

Alice in Wonderland

Tom Sawyer

Little Women

SERIES 741 – LEGENDS

Aladdin & his wonderful lamp

Ali Baba & the forty thieves

Famous Legends (Book 2)

Robin Hood

King Arthur and the
Knights of the Round Table

SERIES 742 – FABLES

Aesop's Fables (Book 1)

Aesop's Fables (Book 2)

La Fontaine's Fables:
The Fox turned Wolf

SERIES SL – LARGE FORMAT

Gulliver's Travels

Aesop's Fables

SERIES 872
MYSTERY & ADVENTURE

Ghostly Tales

SERIES 841
HORROR CLASSICS

Dracula

Frankenstein

The Mummy

The strange case of
Dr Jekyll & Mr Hyde

Hound of the Baskervilles

Ladybird titles cover a wide range of subjects and reading ages.
Write for a free illustrated list from the publishers:
LADYBIRD BOOKS LTD Loughborough Leicestershire England
and USA – LADYBIRD BOOKS INC Lewiston Maine 04240